THE CHURNING OF THE O[C...]

THE SAGE, DURVASA*, WAS ROAMING THE EARTH...

...WHEN HE BEHELD, IN THE HANDS OF A FLYING NYMPH, A GARLAND OF HEAVENLY FLOWERS.

SO HEADY WAS THE PERFUME OF THOSE FLOWERS THAT THE SAGE BECAME FRANTIC WITH DESIRE FOR THE GARLAND.

BEAUTIFUL NYMPH! GIVE ME THAT GARLAND, I PRAY YOU!

YOU ARE WELCOME TO IT, MY LORD, FOR YOU ARE CERTAINLY WORTHY OF IT.

THE SAGE TOOK THE GARLAND AND WALKED ON.

* HE IS BELIEVED TO BE A PART REINCARNATION OF SHIVA

BY AND BY HE SAW INDRA, THE LORD OF THE GODS WHO RULES THE THREE WORLDS, APPROACHING.

INDRA WAS SEATED ON THE CELESTIAL ELEPHANT AIRAVATA.

O INDRA! ACCEPT THIS GARLAND FROM WHICH, EVEN NOW, THE BEES ARE COLLECTING SWEET AMBROSIA!

INDRA TOOK IT...

...AND JOKINGLY PLACED IT ON THE BROW OF AIRAVATA.

AIRAVATA, INTOXICATED BY THE FRAGRANCE TOOK HOLD OF THE GARLAND WITH HIS TRUNK...

...AND FLUNG IT TO THE GROUND.

SAGE DURVASA WAS FURIOUS.

O, INDRA, WHAT AN ACT OF FOLLY IS THIS! I PRESENTED YOU A GARLAND WHICH IS THE DWELLING PLACE OF SHREE, THE GODDESS OF FORTUNE. YET YOU HAVE SPURNED IT!

YOU IMAGINE THAT I AM JUST ANOTHER ASCETIC AND HAVE TREATED ME WITH DISRESPECT!

KNOW, THEREFORE, THAT JUST AS YOU HAVE CAST THE GARLAND TO THE GROUND SO ALSO SHALL YOUR POWER AS A RULER CRUMBLE TO THE GROUND!

INDRA WAS APPALLED AT WHAT HE HAD DONE.

DISMOUNTING FROM HIS ELEPHANT HE BOWED HUMBLY BEFORE DURVASA.

SINLESS DURVASA, THIS ACT WAS DONE IN A MOMENT OF WEAKNESS. PLEASE FORGIVE ME!

BUT DURVASA WAS UNYIELDING.

I AM NOT COMPASSIONATE OF HEART, NOR DO I FORGIVE EASILY. I WILL NOT RELENT. YOU WHO ARE SO ARROGANT BY NATURE—DO YOU EXPECT ME TO ACCEPT YOUR NEW-FOUND HUMILITY?

FROM THAT DAY ONWARDS, PLANTS AND HERBS BEGAN TO WITHER. INDRA AND THE GODS LOST THEIR VIGOUR.

I FEEL DRAINED OF ALL ENERGY!

THERE IS NO ZEST IN LIFE ANY MORE!

OH, HOW COULD DURVASA HAVE BEEN SO HARSH!

IN THIS SITUATION, IT WAS THE ASURAS, THE ENEMIES OF THE DEVAS, WHO BENEFITED. THEY TAUNTED THE DEVAS.

YOU PROUD AND ARROGANT DEVAS! COME, FIGHT WITH US!

SO YOU HESITATE! WEAKLINGS!

THE DEVAS WERE FORCED TO ACCEPT THE CHALLENGE, THOUGH THEY WERE UNWILLING.

TAKE THAT!

AND THAT!

GREAT NUMBERS OF DEVAS WERE FELLED AND COULD NOT RISE AGAIN. THE REST, HEADED BY AGNI, THE GOD OF FIRE, FLED.

THEY DID NOT STOP TILL THEY CAME TO THE REGIONS OF BRAHMA.

OH, HOW WEAK AND TIRED I FEEL!

BRAHMA'S COURT WAS ON THE CREST OF THE SHINING MOUNT MERU. IT WAS FULL OF GRACEFUL TREES, FRAGRANT FLOWERS AND COOL STREAMS. BUT THE DEVAS WERE NOT SOOTHED EVEN BY THE SOFT BREEZE.

NOTHING INTERESTS ME ANY MORE, NOT EVEN THE MELODIOUS SINGING OF THE BIRDS!

THEY NOW APPROACHED BRAHMA.

O BRAHMA, LORD OF ALL CREATIONS, PLEASE SAVE US! TELL US WHAT TO DO AND WE WILL CERTAINLY DO IT. ONLY FREE US FROM SAGE DURVASA'S CURSE.

BRAHMA WAS MOVED BY THEIR SAD PLIGHT. HE MEDITATED FOR A WHILE...

...AND REMEMBERED THE OMNIPOTENT VISHNU.

THEN— LET US SEEK THE HELP OF THE ONE, TO WHOM ALL THE GODS, THE ASURAS, THE ANIMALS, THE BIRDS, TREES AND EVEN I MYSELF... OWE OUR EXISTENCE. LET US SEEK VISHNU'S HELP.

COME, I WILL TAKE YOU TO HIM MYSELF.

WHEN BRAHMA HIMSELF LEADS US, HOW CAN WE FAIL!

WHEN THEY ARRIVED IN VAIKUNTHA, THE ABODE OF VISHNU, SO DAZZLED WERE THEY BY HIS BRILLIANCE, THAT THEY COULD NOT SEE THE FORM OF THE LORD.

WE BOW TO YOU...

WE BOW TO YOU UNCHANGING ONE...!

THE DEVAS WORSHIPPED VISHNU.

O THOU FOREMOST OF THE PURUSHAS!

OH, THOU ALL-KNOWING ONE!

FINALLY THEY WERE ABLE TO SEE HIM. HE WAS AS LUSTROUS AS A THOUSAND SUNS.

O, ALL-KNOWING BEING, SINCE NOTHING REMAINS HIDDEN FROM YOU, NEITHER PAST NOR PRESENT, YOU KNOW OF OUR PLIGHT.

HELP US THEREFORE AND GIVE US VICTORY AGAINST THE ASURAS.

LORD VISHNU WAS SILENT FOR A WHILE, THEN—

LISTEN TO ME CAREFULLY AND ALL WILL BE WELL WITH YOU.

YOUR ENEMIES HAVE OBTAINED VICTORY OVER YOU. SO, FOR THE MOMENT, YOU MUST MAKE PEACE WITH THEM.

HOW CAN WE DO THAT? THEY TAKE UNFAIR ADVANTAGE OF US AT EVERY TURN.

IT IS BETTER TO MAKE PEACE WITH ENEMIES, EVEN AS A SERPENT WILL MAKE FRIENDS WITH A MOUSE, IF NECESSARY.

BUT, LORD, WE ARE AFRAID TO GO NEAR THEM!

THAT IS WHY I SAY YOU MUST FIRST MAKE PEACE WITH THEM. THEN YOU MUST ENDEAVOUR TO CHURN UP THE NECTAR OF IMMORTALITY FROM THE OCEAN.

GET THOSE VERY ASURAS TO HELP YOU TO OBTAIN IT. ONCE YOU HAVE PARTAKEN OF IT, YOU WILL HAVE NOTHING TO FEAR FROM THEM EVER AGAIN!

BUT THEN, IF THE ASURAS HELP US WITH THE CHURNING, WON'T THEY ALSO HAVE THE ADVANTAGE OF THE NECTAR?

NO! THOUGH THEY WILL HELP WITH THE CHURNING, THE NECTAR WILL NOT BE THEIRS!

THE DEVAS WERE PLEASED WITH VISHNU'S ADVICE. THEY BOWED IN REVERENCE TO HIM.

WE WILL INVITE THE ASURAS TO JOIN US IN CHURNING THE OCEAN.

THE DEVAS WENT TO BALI, THE KING OF THE ASURAS. HE WAS RESTING AFTER HAVING CONQUERED THE THREE WORLDS.

LOOK AT THOSE WEAKLINGS, BEREFT OF ARMOUR AND WEAPONS!

LET'S STRIKE THEM DOWN!

NO! DO NOT DRAW YOUR WEAPONS. IT IS TIME TO MAKE PEACE WITH OUR ENEMIES.

BESIDES THEY OBVIOUSLY HAVE SOMETHING TO SAY TO US. SOME SCHEME FOR OUR MUTUAL BENEFIT PERHAPS?

SPEAK! WHY HAVE YOU COME HERE, AT GREAT RISK TO YOURSELVES? HAVE YOU SOME PROPOSALS TO MAKE?

WE HAVE, O WISE AND ILLUSTRIOUS KING!

WELL, GO ON THEN.

FIRST TELL US— ARE YOU INTERESTED IN OBTAINING THE CELESTIAL NECTAR, THE DRINK THAT IMPARTS IMMORTALITY?

THE CELESTIAL NECTAR!

HE'S ASKING US IF WE WOULD LIKE TO HAVE THE NECTAR!

OF COURSE, WE HAVE ALWAYS BEEN INTERESTED BUT EVERYONE KNOWS IT IS ALMOST IMPOSSIBLE TO OBTAIN IT.

WELL, WE HAVE DISCOVERED THE WAY TO DO IT. FIRST OF COURSE WE HAVE TO CHURN THE OCEAN OF MILK...

HERE IS OUR PLAN. WILL YOU HELP US?

HMMM... A GOOD PLAN. VERY INTERESTING!

BALI DISCUSSED THE PLAN WITH OTHER ASURA LEADERS, SHAMBARA, ARISHTANEMI, PAULOMA AND KALAKEYA.

DON'T YOU THINK THE PLAN IS A GOOD ONE?

YES, IT IS.

SO, FOR THE MOMENT, THE DEVAS AND THE ASURAS MADE A CONTRACT OF FRIENDSHIP.

LET US START MAKING OUR PREPARATIONS.

THEY WENT TOGETHER TO THE OCEAN OF MILK...

...AND THEY CAST ALL SORTS OF MEDICINAL HERBS INTO IT.

WE ARE READY, BUT THE OCEAN IS LIKE A MIGHTY CHURNING POT. WHAT SHALL WE CHURN IT WITH?

ONLY A MOUNTAIN WOULD DO AS A CHURNING ROD!

LORD VISHNU TOLD US TO UPROOT MOUNT MANDARA FOR THIS PURPOSE.

THAT'S RIGHT.

LET'S TRY AND UPROOT MOUNT MANDARA AND USE IT AS A CHURNING ROD.

THE MAJESTIC MOUNT MANDARA ADORNED WITH CLOUD-TOPPED PEAKS EXTENDED ELEVEN THOUSAND YOJANAS ABOVE THE GROUND AND WAS AS DEEPLY EMBEDDED IN THE EARTH.

INDRA AND THE DEVAS ALONG WITH BALI AND THE ASURAS UPROOTED MOUNT MANDARA...

...AND BEGAN TO CARRY IT TOWARDS THE OCEAN. ALTHOUGH THEY WERE VERY STRONG, THEY PANTED AND GASPED UNDER ITS WEIGHT.

IT'S SO HEAVY!

OH! WHY DID WE EVER EMBARK ON THIS PROJECT?

ON AND ON THEY WENT, OVER A GREAT DISTANCE.

OH! I AM EXHAUSTED! I CANNOT GO ANY FARTHER.

NOR... I!

OR I!

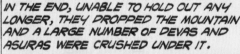

IN THE END, UNABLE TO HOLD OUT ANY LONGER, THEY DROPPED THE MOUNTAIN AND A LARGE NUMBER OF DEVAS AND ASURAS WERE CRUSHED UNDER IT.

THE CRIES OF THE ASURAS AND DEVAS INTERMINGLED.

HELP!

HELP!

WHAT SHALL WE DO NOW?

WE ARE NOWHERE NEAR COMPLETION OF OUR TASK!

BOTH THE ASURAS AND THE DEVAS WERE IN DESPAIR.

SO MANY OF OUR FRIENDS HAVE BEEN CRUSHED AND INJURED!

BUT LORD VISHNU, WHO SAW ALL THIS, ARRIVED ON HIS VEHICLE, GARUDA.

IT'S LORD VISHNU!

LORD VISHNU!

HIS HEALING GLANCE FELL ON THEM, AND THE INJURED DEVAS AND ASURAS WERE REVIVED.

OH, PAULOMA! YOU ARE WELL AGAIN!

OH, AGNI! HOW GLAD I AM TO SEE YOU ABLE TO STAND UP AGAIN!

THEN LORD VISHNU EFFORTLESSLY RAISED THE MOUNTAIN WITH ONE HAND...

...AND PLACED IT ON THE BACK OF GARUDA.

VISHNU HIMSELF THEN MOUNTED GARUDA AND PROCEEDED TOWARDS THE OCEAN OF MILK.

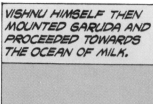

ON REACHING THERE, GARUDA GENTLY PLACED THE MOUNTAIN IN THE OCEAN...

...AND THEN FLEW AWAY. LORD VISHNU REMAINED BEHIND.

THEN THE DEVAS AND ASURAS WENT TO VASUKI, THE KING OF THE SNAKES.

O, VASUKI, COME HELP US TO CHURN THE MIGHTY OCEAN AND YOU SHALL ALSO PARTAKE OF THE NECTAR.

CERTAINLY! I WILL COME AND ACT AS A CHURNING ROPE.

SO VASUKI WENT WITH THEM AND ALLOWED THEM TO BIND HIM ROUND MOUNT MANDARA.

BUT ALAS! THERE WAS NO SUPPORT UNDER MOUNT MANDARA AND BECAUSE OF ITS IMMENSE WEIGHT, IT GRADUALLY SLIPPED DOWN TO THE BOTTOM OF THE OCEAN.

THE MOUNTAIN WON'T TURN!

THE MOUNTAIN IS SLIPPING FROM OUR GRASP!

NO! IT IS SLIPPING DOWN DEEPER AND DEEPER.

HELP! HELP!

ONCE AGAIN VISHNU CAME TO THEIR AID. ASSUMING THE FORM OF A GIGANTIC TORTOISE, ALMOST LIKE A HUGE ISLAND, VISHNU DIVED TO THE BOTTOM OF THE OCEAN...

...AND HELD MOUNT MANDARA UP ON HIS BACK.

BEGIN THE CHURNING!

THROUGH THE GRACE OF LORD VISHNU, THE DEVAS AND THE ASURAS AND VASUKI FELT A RENEWED STRENGTH WITHIN THEM AND THEY CHURNED FASTER AND FASTER.

THEN FIRE AND SMOKE ISSUED FROM THE THOUSAND MOUTHS OF VASUKI.

THESE FIERY PUFFS OF SMOKE ENGULFED THE ASURAS WHO WERE NEAR THE HOODS OF THE SNAKE.

I CAN'T BREATHE!

THESE FUMES ARE SUFFOCATING US!

LOOK! ALL OUR GREAT LEADERS PAULOMA, KALEYA, ILVALA SO PALE AND FAINT! THEY LOOK LIKE SHRIVELLED SHRUBS BURNT DOWN BY A FOREST FIRE!

THE DEVAS TOO WERE AFFECTED BY THE FUMES, BUT VISHNU SENT DOWN COOLING SHOWERS TO REVIVE THEM.

STILL THE DEVAS AND ASURAS CONTINUED THEIR TASK AND AS THEY CHURNED, A WHOLE HOST OF FISHES, SNAKES, WHALES WERE CHURNED UP TOO.

THEN THERE AROSE A FEARFUL POISON. IT SPREAD LIKE A THICK PALL OVER THE EARTH.

THIS IS THE TERRIBLE POISON, HALAHALA!

IT WILL SOON COVER THE WORLD AND KILL ALL ITS CREATURES!

THIS TIME THEY SENT UP A CRY TO LORD SHIVA —

LORD SHIVA WE ARE DYING! PLEASE HELP US!

INSTANTLY SHIVA HEEDED THEIR CALL, GATHERING UP ALL THE POISON IN THE PALM OF HIS HAND...

...HE SWALLOWED IT AND HELD IT IN HIS THROAT.

THE POISON MADE HIS THROAT BLUE AND BECAME AN ORNAMENT OF SHIVA. FROM THAT TIME ON HE HE HAS BEEN KNOWN AS NILAKANTHA.

WE SALUTE YOU, O NILAKANTHA, FOR RESPONDING TO OUR PRAYER!

THE DEVAS AND ASURAS RESUMED THEIR CHURNING. BEFORE LONG THERE AROSE FROM THE OCEAN SURABHI, THE DIVINE COW, UCHCHHAISHRAVA, THE HORSE WHITE AS THE MOON AND AIRAVATA, THE WHITE ELEPHANT WITH FOUR TUSKS. THEY WERE FOLLOWED BY A BEVY OF BEAUTIFUL APSARAS. LATER EMERGED THE CELESTIAL PARIJATA TREE AND VARUNI THE GODDESS OF WINE, ROLLING HER INTOXICATING EYES.

THEN **SHREE** AROSE FROM THE OCEAN, GRACEFUL AND EFFULGENT.

HER BEAUTY WAS SUCH AS TO STIR THE MINDS OF THE DEVAS AND ASURAS. ALL OF THEM WERE ANXIOUS TO BE OF SERVICE TO HER.

GANGA AND OTHER HOLY RIVERS BROUGHT WATER IN GOLDEN JARS FOR HER ABLUTIONS.

VASANTA, THE GOD OF SPRING, BROUGHT FRUITS AND FLOWERS.

THE APSARAS BEGAN TO DANCE FOR HER.

THE CLOUDS RAINED MUSIC FROM A VARIETY OF INSTRUMENTS.

VARUNA, LORD OF THE WATERS, BROUGHT HER THE CELEBRATED VAIJAYANTI GARLAND.

WHEN THE AUSPICIOUS CEREMONIES WERE COMPLETED, SHREE MOVED HERE AND THERE LOOKING FOR THE ONE WHO IS THE REPOSITORY OF ALL GOOD QUALITIES.

IN THE END, SHE CHOSE LORD VISHNU, WHO IS PERFECT IN EVERY WAY.

SHE PLACED THE BEAUTIFUL VAIJAYANTI GARLAND ROUND HIS NECK.

VISHNU, LORD OF THE THREE WORLDS, ACCEPTED HER.

THE CHURNING CONTINUED.

WHIRR—WHIRR!

FINALLY DHANVANTARI, THE DIVINE PHYSICIAN, CAME FORTH, HOLDING THE VESSEL OF CELESTIAL NECTAR.

AT LAST! THE DIVINE ELIXIR!

THE ASURAS GAVE A GREAT ROAR...

...AND TOOK THE PRECIOUS VESSEL FROM HIM BY FORCE.

ALL IS LOST. O, LORD VISHNU, SAVE THE PRECIOUS NECTAR!

VISHNU AT ONCE ASSUMED THE BEWITCHING FORM OF MOHINI, THE ENCHANTRESS.

MEANWHILE, THE ASURAS HAD BEGUN QUARRELLING AMONG THEMSELVES OVER THE JAR OF NECTAR.

SUDDENLY, THEY SAW MOHINI APPROACHING THEM WITH SWEET LOOKS AND ENCHANTING SMILES.

INTOXICATED WITH HER BEAUTY, THE ASURAS BEGAN TO FOLLOW HER.

SUCH GRACE!

SHE'S BEAUTIFUL!

WHY DON'T WE ASK HER TO DISTRIBUTE THE NECTAR TO US?

MOHINI DECIDED TO TEASE THEM A LITTLE.

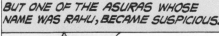

BUT ONE OF THE ASURAS WHOSE NAME WAS RAHU, BECAME SUSPICIOUS.

SHE HAS NO INTENTION OF GIVING US THE NECTAR!

SO RAHU ASSUMED THE FORM OF DEVA AND QUIETLY CROSSED OVER.

FORTUNATELY, SURYA, THE SUN, AND SOMA, THE MOON, WERE WATCHFUL.

WAIT! HE'S NOT A DEVA!

NO, NO, I KNOW HIM! HE IS THE ASURA, RAHU!

THE NECTAR HAD BARELY REACHED RAHU'S THROAT. INSTANTLY VISHNU HURLED HIS CHAKRA AT HIM TO CUT OFF THE WELL-ADORNED HEAD OF THE ASURA.

AS THE HUGE HEADLESS TRUNK OF THE ASURA FELL DOWN, IT CAUSED THE EARTH TO QUAKE AND THE MOUNTAINS TO RUMBLE.

AND THE SEVERED HEAD OF THE ASURA ROSE TO THE SKY ROARING HORRIBLY.

TO THIS DAY THERE IS A DEADLY FEUD BETWEEN THE HEAD OF RAHU AND THE SUN AND THE MOON AND HE SWALLOWS THEM UP AT REGULAR INTERVALS, CAUSING ECLIPSES.

AT LAST, THE TRUTH DAWNED ON THE ASURAS!

THAT'S NO ENCHANTRESS! THAT'S VISHNU!

WE'VE BEEN TRICKED!

THEY BEGAN TO SCREAM AND MAKE A TERRIFIC DIN.

GIVE US THE NECTAR!

IT'S OURS!

AMID GREAT TUMULT AND EXCITEMENT MANY MORE OF THE GODS QUICKLY PARTOOK OF THE NECTAR WHICH THEY SO GREATLY DESIRED AND THEY BECAME IMMORTAL.

MEANWHILE THE ASURAS HAD BEEN ARMING THEMSELVES WITH VARIOUS WEAPONS.

THEN, ON THE SHORES OF THE OCEAN, BEGAN THE GREAT BATTLE BETWEEN THE DEVAS AND THE ASURAS.

SHARP POINTED JAVELINS AND LANCES WERE HURLED AT THE ASURAS.

THE ASURAS DIED IN LARGE NUMBERS THEIR HEADS ADORNED WITH BRIGHT GOLD FELL ON THE FIELD OF BATTLE.

WAR CRIES AND CRIES OF PAIN INTERMINGLED.

ATTACK!

PIERCE!

CUT!

KILL! KILL!

AT THE HEIGHT OF THIS FIERCE BATTLE, VISHNU ENTERED THE FIELD.

THEY SEEM EVENLY MATCHED. THE DEVAS NEED MY HELP.

AS SOON AS HE THOUGHT OF IT, HIS OWN INCOMPARABLE DISCUS, THE SHINING SUDARSHANA CHAKRA, CAME THROUGH THE SKY.

VISHNU AIMED THE SUDHARSHANA AT THE ASURAS. IT FLEW EVERYWHERE DESTROYING THOUSANDS OF ASURAS.

AT OTHER TIMES, IT BLAZED LIKE FIRE AND BURNED EVERYTHING AROUND IT.

BUT THE ASURAS WERE NOT YET DAUNTED. THEY ROSE SKYWARDS...

...AND HURLED HUGE MOUNTAINS AT THE DEVAS.

THE MOUNTAINS COLLIDING WITH EACH OTHER PRODUCED A TREMENDOUS UPROAR.

THE EARTH AND THE FORESTS BEGAN TO TREMBLE.

AGAIN THE DIVINE VISHNU CAME TO THE AID OF THE DEVAS. SHOOTING GOLDEN-HEADED ARROWS AT THE FALLING MOUNTAINS, HE REDUCED THEM TO DUST.

THE ASURAS WERE DEFEATED. THEY COULD FIGHT BACK NO MORE. SHRIEKING LOUDLY, SOME OF THEM ENTERED THE BOWELS OF THE EARTH, WHILE...

...OTHERS PLUNGED INTO THE OCEAN.

THE VICTORIOUS DEVAS PUT MOUNT MANDARA BACK IN ITS OLD PLACE AND DID OBEISANCE TO IT.

THEN THE SKIES RESOUNDED WITH JOYOUS SHOUTS AS THE DEVAS, HAVING BEEN RENDERED PERFECT AFTER DRINKING THE CELESTIAL NECTAR, RETURNED TO THEIR OWN ABODES.

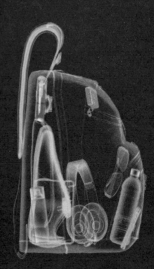